DOUBLE TROUBLE
in Walla Walla

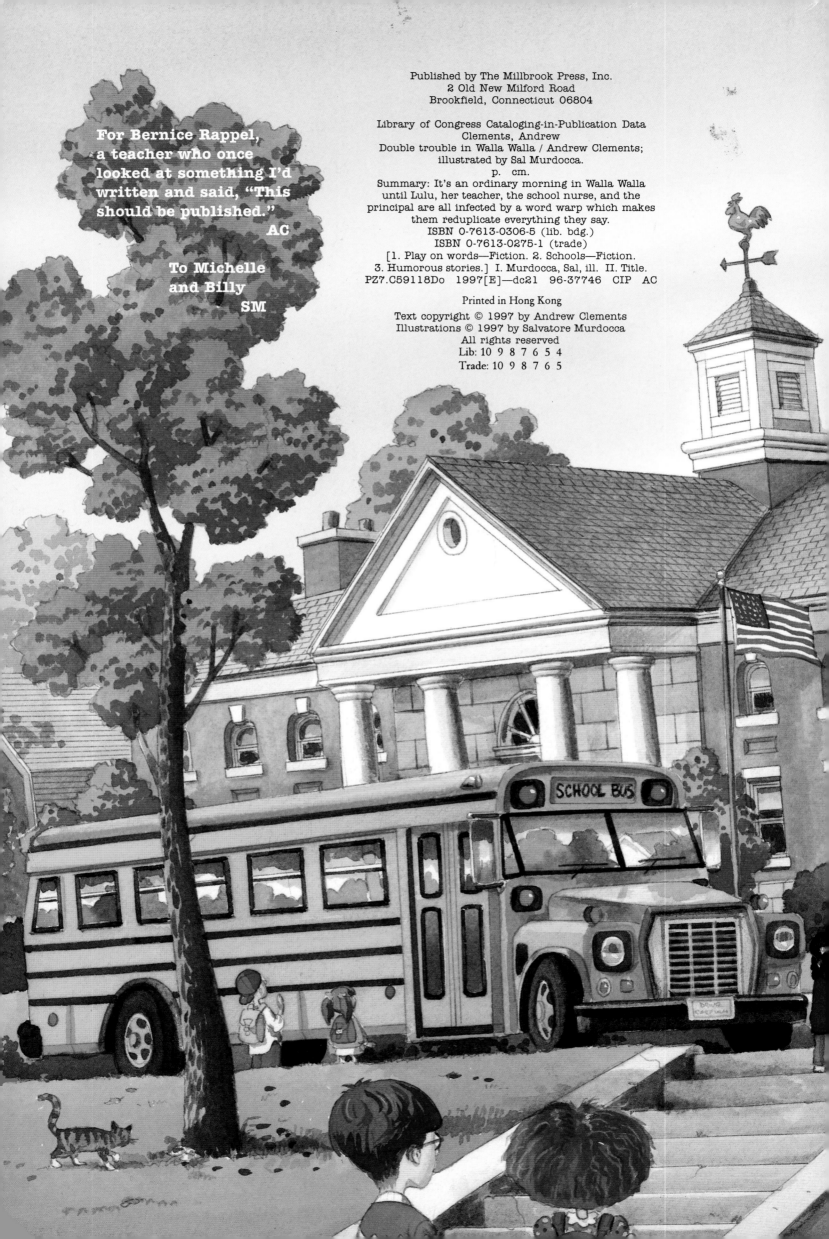

Published by The Millbrook Press, Inc.
2 Old New Milford Road
Brookfield, Connecticut 06804

Library of Congress Cataloging-in-Publication Data
Clements, Andrew
Double trouble in Walla Walla / Andrew Clements;
illustrated by Sal Murdocca.
p. cm.
Summary: It's an ordinary morning in Walla Walla
until Lulu, her teacher, the school nurse, and the
principal are all infected by a word warp which makes
them reduplicate everything they say.
ISBN 0-7613-0306-5 (lib. bdg.)
ISBN 0-7613-0275-1 (trade)
[1. Play on words—Fiction. 2. Schools—Fiction.
3. Humorous stories.] I. Murdocca, Sal, ill. II. Title.
PZ7.C59118Do 1997[E]—dc21 96-37746 CIP AC

Printed in Hong Kong

Text copyright © 1997 by Andrew Clements
Illustrations © 1997 by Salvatore Murdocca
Lib: 10 9 8 7 6 5 4
Trade: 10 9 8 7 6 5

For Bernice Rappel,
a teacher who once
looked at something I'd
written and said, "This
should be published."
AC

To Michelle
and Billy
SM

DOUBLE TROUBLE

in Walla Walla

By Andrew Clements
Illustrated by Sal Murdocca

The Millbrook Press
Brookfield, Connecticut

It was an ordinary Monday morning in Walla Walla—
until Lulu raised her hand in class.

"Mrs. Bell, I feel like a nit-wit. My homework is all higgledy-piggledy. Last night it was in tip-top shape, but now it's a big mish-mash."

Mrs. Bell said, "Nit-wit? Higgledy-piggledy? Mish-mash? Lulu, stop that flip-flop chitter-chatter or you'll be in double trouble!"

Lulu said, "But I'm not trying to flip-flop chit-chat. I just have an itty-bitty problem with my homework."

Mrs. Bell scowled. "All right for you, Lulu. If you're going to shilly-shally and dilly-dally with all this fancy-schmancy yak-yak, then we'll just have to trit-trot down to the principal's office."

Mrs. Bell hurried Lulu down the hall, and they burst into the principal's office.

Mr. Thomas said, "What's all the hubbub about?"

Mrs. Bell said, "Lulu's been trying to razzle-dazzle me with some kind of lippity-loppity jibber-jabber, and now I'm all helter-skelter myself!"

Mr. Thomas raised his eyebrows. "Tut-tut, sounds like silly-willy hocus-pocus to me."

Mrs. Bell's mouth dropped open. She pointed to the principal and said "Eeeka-freaka! Lulu's got your tongue all topsy-turvy too!"

"Now, now, don't get the jim-jams, Mrs. Bell. Let's give the nurse a yoo-hoo." Mr. Thomas picked up his phone and said, "Mrs. Carter, I'm going to pitter-patter over to your office, okey-dokey?"

. . . okey-dokey?

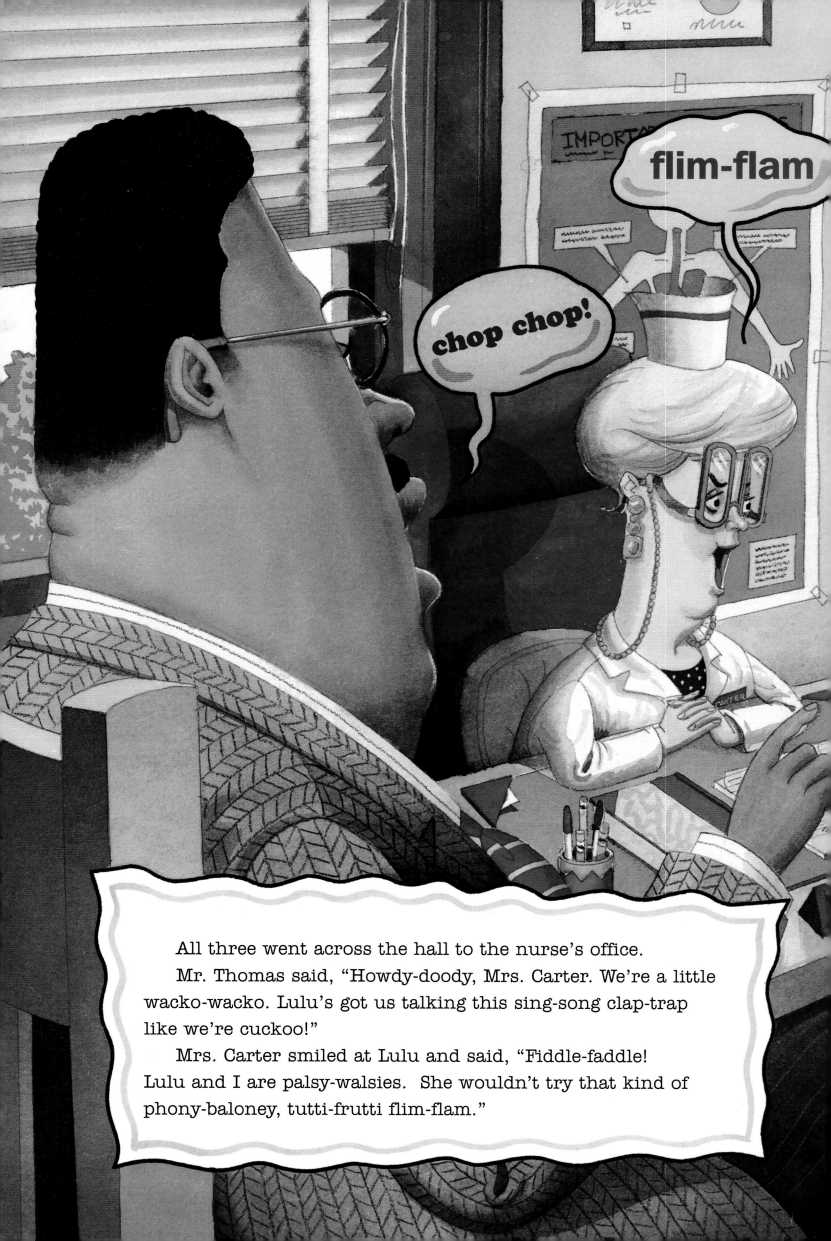

All three went across the hall to the nurse's office.

Mr. Thomas said, "Howdy-doody, Mrs. Carter. We're a little wacko-wacko. Lulu's got us talking this sing-song clap-trap like we're cuckoo!"

Mrs. Carter smiled at Lulu and said, "Fiddle-faddle! Lulu and I are palsy-walsies. She wouldn't try that kind of phony-baloney, tutti-frutti flim-flam."

Lulu and her teacher and the principal stared at the nurse.

Lulu said, "Wowie-zowie!"

Mrs. Bell said, "Jeepers-creepers!"

And Mr. Thomas said, "Holy-moly! You're in the same hodge-podge we are! I'd better give the superintendent a jingle-jangle—chop chop!"

"Wait one ding-dang tick-tock!" shouted the nurse. "If you chit-chat with the big-wig, then he'll yak-yak like Lulu too! If we're not very, very hush-hush about this, there could be a mongo-mongo brain-drain, and everybody in Walla Walla will be talking like a herky-jerky ding-a-ling!"

Then the nurse turned to Lulu. "Lulu, let's get to the nitty-gritty: When did all this mumbo-jumbo start?"

Lulu gulped. She said, "In English class I had an itsy-bitsy problem with my homework, and then— zip-zap—Mrs. Bell said talking like this was a no-no."

The nurse looked over the top of her glasses at Lulu. "Something like this would not just happen willy-nilly. Now Lulu, think extra, extra hard, and tell me what you did yesterday."

Mrs. Carter said, "Lulu, it seems to me that you've opened up a knock'em sock'em wibble-wobble word warp! I usually don't believe in this kind of hoodoo bunko-junko, but if it was going to happen anywhere, it would probably happen right here in Walla Walla!"

Mrs. Bell said, "Let's not quibble-quabble, Mrs. Carter. I'm getting the heebie-jeebies from all this razzmatazz! What can we do?"

Walla Walla!

"We should say all the rootin'-tootin', crink'em-crank'em, woolly-bully words we can think of. Maybe that will clear the air and close the warp! Worth a try?" asked Nurse Carter.

Mr. Thomas said, "Aye-aye!"

Mrs. Bell said, "Let's do-si-do!"

And Lulu said, "Uh-huh!"

Nurse Carter closed the door to her office. Then she turned around and said, "Lulu, let's get this harum-scarum show on the road!"

And then, suddenly, silence.

Lulu, Mrs. Bell, and Mr. Thomas slumped into chairs, and Mrs. Carter flopped onto the cot against the wall.

Was it over? No one dared to speak.

Lulu whispered, "Mrs. Carter, may I please have a drink of water?"

Mrs. Carter sat up and said, "Of course you may, dear."

Mrs. Bell smiled weakly at the principal and said, "You were magnificent, sir."

Mr. Thomas perked up and smiled at everyone. He straightened his tie and said, "I think we've done it, people!"

Mrs. Carter sat down at her desk and went back to checking over her posture records. Mr. Thomas walked across the hall to his office and went back to the letter he was writing. Lulu followed Mrs. Bell down the hallway and soon had her English homework all straightened out.

And after English it was just an ordinary Monday in Walla Walla.

Things we like
Word Games
Breakfast
cereal
Lunch
Dinner
Teams
Blue 4
Red 0
White 2
hobnob
mayday
"Ta-ta, Lulu."
"Bye-bye, Mrs. Ding-Dong."